KT-154-818

TALES FROM SOUTH LONDON

Edited By Lottie Boreham

First published in Great Britain in 2017 by:

Young Writers
Remus House
Coltsfoot Drive
Peterborough
PE2 9BF
Telephone: 01733 890066
Website: www.youngwriters.co.uk

All Rights Reserved
Book Design by Spencer Hart
© Copyright Contributors 2017
SB ISBN 978-1-78820-177-3
Printed and bound in the UK by BookPrintingUK
Website: www.bookprintinguk.com
YB0321F

FOREWORD

Welcome Reader!

Are you ready to discover weird and wonderful creatures from the wildest depths of your imagination?

For Young Writers' latest competition we asked primary school pupils nationwide to create a crazy creature of their own invention and include it in a mini saga of 100 words or less; a difficult task indeed! However, they have risen to the challenge magnificently and the resulting collection contains a plethora of fearsome monsters and awesome aliens.

Here at Young Writers our aim is to encourage creativity in children and to inspire a love of the written word, so it is fantastic to receive such an amazing response, with some completely imaginative and brilliant stories. Not only have these young writers created entirely unique and interesting creatures, they have also crafted wonderful tales to showcase their creations. These stories are brimming with inspiration, from mysterious monsters battling in new worlds, to out-of-this-world alien altercations!

I'd like to congratulate all the young authors in 'Crazy Creatures - Tales From South London - I hope this inspires them to continue with their creative writing.

Lottie Boreham

CONTENTS

Maddie-Lee Reader-Penfold (9) 63
Aaron Ellery (9) 64
Maddie Louise Darby (11) 65
Amelisa Mucaj (10) 66
Joel Adjei Twum (7) 67
Aaron Kamina (8) 68
Victoria Oluwasemilore 69
Abdul (10)
Davina Olukoko (10) 70
Tyler Jerome Newman (10) 71
Damilola Mosuro (10) 72
Rubie Nicole Worf (8) 73
Chiamaka Udochuku Obosi (11) 74

Henwick Primary School, Eltham

Lizzie Herelle-Savage (8) 75
Melanie Stoyanova (8) 76
Viktoria Marinusovna 77
Broeren (8)
Theadora Burke (8) 78
Ismail Cemil Ustundag (8) 79
Maddie Foley (8) 80
Yezda Demirkol (8) 81
Mia Vuckovic (9) 82
Jesse Ku (9) 83
Sonny Godbolt (9) 84
Nevaeh Conteh (9) 85
Bobby Patrick George Tolley (8) 86

St Anselm's Catholic Primary School, Wandsworth

Sebastian Recordon (8) 87
Benjamin Wevill (8) 88
Ella Lewis (8) 89
Gianluca Pietro Acanfora (9) 90
Victoria Alexandra 91
Pajaczkowska (9)
Ruby Cox (9) 92
Niamh Worrell (9) 93
Elizabeth Ilona Anghenica (9) 94
Joseph Awad (9) 95
Maria Ikpase (8) 96

Riley Jein (8) 97
Gene Allaway (9) 98
Rafael Das (9) 99
Shauna Murney (8) 100
Elizabeth Margaret Patricia 101
Armitage (9)
Chloé Sachet-Dufraisse (8) 102
Cormac Haspel (8) 103
Johnny Gardner (9) 104
Thomas Hulett (8) 105
Blanche Symington (8) 106
Raphaelle Olivia Treneman (8) 107
Marianne Amate (9) 108
Ava Boaten (9) 109
Finn Mulcahy (9) 110
Isabel Stahel (9) 111
Thomas Pike (8) 112
Alfie Henry Pennington (9) 113
Charles Wilson (9) 114

St Helen's RC Primary School, Brixton

Kolade Alli (10) 115
Samuel O Ajayi (9) 116
Lillyrose Tuswa (9) 117
Jaden Frempong (10) 118
Henok Ghebrihiwot Tecle (10) 119
Olubisi Olubode (10) 120
Asia Mieszczakowska (10) 121
Blanca Santeugini (10) 122
Mya Pontes (10) 123
Justin Dafê (10) 124
Jean Yves Dorgeles Zehia (10) 125
Sean Diego Encalada 126
Obaco (10)
Luis Coelho (10) 127

St Mary Magdalen's Catholic Primary School, London

Bill McCarthy (8) 128
Lavinia Cora Fia Hopkins (9) 129
Lukas Glasheen (9) 130

Edward Jones (9)   131
Brisa Willoughby (9)   132
Maaira Hussain (9)   133
Saoirse Chandler (8)   134
Sadhbh Fahy (8)   135
David William Derfinak (9)   136
Elliot Laurence Kinsella (8)   137
Shane Kenny (8)   138
TJ Maciejewski (9)   139
Maja Paliga (9)   140
Tonatiuh Fiorini (9)   141
Samiha Sohail (8)   142
Tyler Davidson Wanjiru (9)   143

St Olave's Preparatory School, New Eltham

Emily Sophia Lysons (10)   144
Emilia Grace Morgan (10)   145
Adam Barbe (9)   146
Mia Alexandra Wilks (8)   147
Ajmal Malique (9)   148
Zuriel Elueme (9)   149
Darcey Baxter (9)   150
Rania Kochhar (10)   151
Mia Griffiths (10)   152
Qasim Ahmed (9)   153
Ethan Daley (10)   154
Sophia Zoryana Smith (10)   155
Sofia Chhatlani (9)   156
Mia-Rainbow O'Regan (9)   157
Henry Wygas (10)   158
Matthew Pownall (9)   159
Harry James Green (10)   160
Christopher Thomas (10)   161
Ben Fowler (10)   162
Dhillon Blaggan (10)   163

THE STORIES

Sometimes You Have To Make A Change

Maan stood in the park taking pictures of his surroundings, whilst receiving dirty looks from 'those strange humans', as he called them.

'Maan,' said his master, Humaan, through Maan's earpiece, 'Enter a bathroom and transform into a puppy?'

'Yes.'

'Thanks. In this form you will pretend to be a stray and a stupid, unsuspecting human will take you to their home. Then you can observe the strange ways of the human race. Now let's begin!'

As Maan stepped outside, someone spotted him.

'Call the pest control!' screamed the woman.

'Flipit bork!' said Maan or, in his language, 'Oh no!'

Gabriel Baptise Halliday (10)

Clapham Manor Primary School, Clapham

The Race To Safety

Floyd leapt over the blooming berry bushes as his extending legs grabbed the dirt in front of him, and pulled him forward. Something was behind him but he kept on running. He knew that any wild creature couldn't reach Thumbtopia.

'It's there, it's there!' shouted Floyd excitedly as his purple and orange spots shone across the trees with excitement.

He finally realised that the creature was five metres closer than it was twenty seconds ago. Floyd's legs ran faster and faster He could almost touch Thumbtopia. *Crash!* The creature and Floyd scrambled to Thumbtopia. Push, shove and Floyd was safe.

Lola Vivi Sacerdote (10)
Clapham Manor Primary School, Clapham

Friends Across The Galaxy!

'Bye Blobaglob!' screamed the creatures of Neptune, 'Have fun on Earth, make connections.' Once it landed on Earth, it was confused. Soon, Nice-Guy took Blobaglob into his house.

The next day, Blobaglob was on the TV, in a lab, with a scientist. The scientist wanted to see inside this creature. Nice-Guy was not happy, he raced down the street to save the Blobaglob. The Blobaglob was scared. The doors flew open, the wind played with Nice-Guy's hair.

'I am taking it home.'

Nice-Guy grabbed Blobaglob and took him home. Blobaglob returned with friends across the galaxy. Hooray, yeah!

Zeinab Sabri (10)

Clapham Manor Primary School, Clapham

The Carkkoss Who Faced Her Fears...

A lovely, young Carkkoss was flying through the Rocky Mountains. She was suddenly attacked by an Arrane and badly wounded. When she awoke, she called her friends to help her find the vicious beast who left her for dead.

After six days of searching, they found something very suspicious, a large rock that had a huge torch hanging from this strange latch. The Carkkoss went inside... and found mountains of gold and jewels. Then she saw it; the Arrane who attacked her. He flew down with a group of Sandcrocs who looked smaller than they should've been. Then it started...

Jacob Pempelfort Sherwin (9)
Clapham Manor Primary School, Clapham

Bobalobatob Vs Jeff

Bob crept out of bed with Alob and Atob trailing behind. When, eventually, Alob and Atob woke up, the process sped up a lot. Once, they were at the door, Bob used the force on his antennae to open the door vigorously. Trudging through the snow, they heard a faint hissing. It was recognised instantly as a Jeff. Bob and Atob turned back, petrified, but the power of Alob was unstoppable. Alob's eyes were bubbling, Bob was cowering but before they knew it, Alob had destroyed the beast wonderfully. Alob had bravely saved the day. Bobalobatob lived happily ever after.

Pebbles Love Doughty-White (9)
Clapham Manor Primary School, Clapham

The Massacurra

In a jungle, deep in South America, there lies a half human, half creature, who's hardly ever seen, but known too well by the natives. It has scales all over, and a huge head to hold its red, petrifying eyes. It lingers on land and water, and calls into the night to lure victims. Its last recorded prey was a man from Austria called Havärd Osa, who was reported hiking through the jungle looking for snakes. The Massacurra had slaughtered Havärd to death, slicing his limbs with a sharpened branch and stones. His body remains along with a close-by howling.

Shakiràh Farinha (9)
Clapham Manor Primary School, Clapham

Curlynob's Trip To Greenie's House

Curlynob set off to go to Greenie's house. Greenie was a monster and they were best friends. They did everything together. On the way, he met Crankypants and Prissy Princess. They were also his friends. He said, 'Hi!' and carried on walking. While he was walking, he tripped over a log. Snakey was under there. Snakey and Curlynob were very good friends. He finally arrived at Greenie's house but he couldn't find him. He wasn't in the house.

Where could he be? Curlynob asked himself. Maybe he was taken, oh dear!

Humaira Ahmed (10)
Clapham Manor Primary School, Clapham

Blob And The Missing Slot

Once upon a time there was a creature called Blob. Blob was a jellified animal that was created by a mad scientist who was messing with goo. Blob's adventure started in a shop that had lots of jelly in it. Blob owned this shop and one day he found a missing jelly. He was terrified that the jelly would form a huge army to teach Blob a lesson for keeping them on shelves. Suddenly, there was a noise of slithering. Blob turned to see a pink, raspberry-flavoured jelly running around. He ran towards it. Faster, faster, almost there. 'Gotcha!'

Gilbert Hare (9)
Clapham Manor Primary School, Clapham

Bob And Jeff

Once upon a time there lived a monster named Bob and a human named Jeff, they were best friends. One day, Tob, Bob's worst enemy, kidnapped Jeff. When Bob heard the news, he went after Tob. He arrived at Tob's secret hideout and demanded he give Jeff back.
Tob said, 'You want Jeff back? Then you'll get me two objects, a bottle of tears and some squid ink. Don't use seawater otherwise I'll explode.'
Bob knew what to do. He got seawater and squid ink. He gave it to Tob. Bob escaped with Jeff whilst Tob exploded.

Sukina Ahad (10)
Clapham Manor Primary School, Clapham

The Last Hobbogoblin On Earth

Typhos arrives and no one's there. He looks everywhere and he finds a letter saying, *Come to London, it's fun, Mum*. He jumps and shoots the spikes out of his body, he shivers at the name of London. He thinks Mum told stories of that place, it seemed scary.

Two days later, he arrives in London and he starts to look for the entire race of the hobbogoblins but it's a big trap for money and he falls right into it! He looks for a mansion on Baley Street, from the letter, but there's men waiting for him, heavily armed...

Keir Gabriel Kakembo (10)

Clapham Manor Primary School, Clapham

New Planet

Oh no! Rapper Zapper had stolen the only flying machine on Planet Reepo. He wrecked his lab and flew off from the colourless world. He used his special detectors on the back of his head and his six brains to tell him if he was chased. This place was spectacular, exploding with a celebration of colours and the sand was the most soft thing he'd tasted in his entire life. Everything on his planet was rock-hard. It was also the most delicious thing although he ate everything. He found a sign saying: *The Sahara Desert*.

Khalid Nurhussien (10)
Clapham Manor Primary School, Clapham

Captured On Holiday

Pity-Moo flew across the evening sky with her bat-shaped wings. A ball of fire with a mop of flowing water for hair, the creature was freezing. This was nothing like a holiday. For one thing, there was no lava swirling around her. Suddenly, there came a cry. Pity-Moo used the small amount of things she knew to work out the cry came from a falcon. The monster was grabbed by a pair of talons and dragged to the ground. The ball shot out a flame of fire and quickly put it out with her hair. The bird was gone.

Nami Ramos (10)
Clapham Manor Primary School, Clapham

Princess Ugly-Emoji's New Friend

She was walking with her worst enemy, Loxie, when she discovered an evil rock so she put the rock in poison water. Loxie got mad, she got angry. She screamed at the princess.
'How dare you!'
'I was just helping,' cried Princess Ugly-Emoji.
'Well, you're not,' Loxie shouted.
'Listen, you need to hear what you're saying. I know you don't mean it,' she replied.
'I know, I'm so sorry,' Loxie whispered sadly.
'It's OK,' Princess said.
She grabbed hold of Loxie's arm. Loxie held it back.
'Friend?' she asked.
'Friends,' replied Princess Ugly-emoji.
Friendship is the best.

Leona Dale (10)
De Lucy Primary School, Abbey Wood

The Staring Contest!

One day, Songnfee was just minding his own business when out jumped Lavansga - the horrible nine-eyed creature made from lava, that lived on the sun.

'What are you doing here?' asked Songnfee, an eight-eyed creature made from fire that lived on Mars.

'Well... I've actually come to challenge you to a competition of your choice,' he exclaimed.

'Ha! You want to challenge me? Sure! Can it be... a staring contest?' he asked slyly.

You see Songnfee was no ordinary creature, he was a staring master!

'Ha! Of course!' exclaimed Lavansga, not knowing Songnfee's plan.

'Perfect. It'll be tomorrow.'

Sophie Jaramillo-Prado (11)
De Lucy Primary School, Abbey Wood

Zika And Zurfa: The Final Prank!

Long ago, in the village of Acresville, lived a positive purple monster named Zika. Surprisingly, this morning she wasn't in the greatest mood. She was huffing and puffing and had a frown on her face. Zurfa, her arch-nemesis, was why she was upset. Zurfa always copied her.

I know what I can do! I'll use my shape-shifting powers to prank her! she thought.

Trotting onwards, she approached Zurfa, in the form of her friend Trella.

'I hate you!' said Trella.

Zurfa caught on.

'I know it's you, Zika!' she bellowed.

Zika apologised; since that day they've never pranked each other.

Sukriti Bhandari (10)
De Lucy Primary School, Abbey Wood

The Monster Who Needed Roarsome Help!

Once, there was a clever but not scary creature. He needed help to be a mean and frightening monster. This monster's street was Sticky Hill and his country was Abialienar. While he was walking on Crazy Road, he met an alien who had sharp, painted horns he looked like a demon. Also his name was Stink Saw.

'Hello,' said Stink Saw.

'Hello,' said Fright Nor, 'can you teach me how to be scary?'

'Yes! First you need to be strong and mean, like this... Hello!' *Burp* and smirk.

'You try,' he said.

'Hello!' *Burp*, smirk!

'Well done.'

'Wow! Yes.'

Abigail Oluwaseyifunmi Olabamidele (7)

De Lucy Primary School, Abbey Wood

The Star Brightness Stealer

Shannon, the shape-shifter, was counting the shimmering stars of the star dimension. Surprisingly, she noticed a less shiny star to investigate, she shape-shifted into a bird and flew to that star. Once she got on to the pale-grey surface of it, she saw a creature sucking its brightness with a machine.

'Hey, what are you doing?' shouted Shannon.

'I was just purifying the brightness of the star,' it answered.

Something seemed suspicious. His eyes glistened like glass. His skin seemed leathery. Suddenly, wind blew his mask.

'You're from the moon dimension!' shouted Shannon.

They knew it was time for trouble.

Lavanya Aggarwal (11)
De Lucy Primary School, Abbey Wood

Night-Time Monsters!

Minos, a bandaged-up monster, who lived in a cave, always asked his mother to check for monsters under the bed. But one night it felt different. His mother left and later in the night, he heard scratches. Minos looked and there was a laser-eyed, stubby monster.

'Arghhhhh!'

'Don't be afraid, I check on you at night.'

Smiling at him with razor-sharp teeth.

'Goodnight!'

She was gone.

'That was strange.'

Startled, he sat in his bed, looking up. Mum leapt in.

'What was all the screaming about?'

'I can't wait for tomorrow night.'

He slept until dawn had broken.

Brooke Erin Priestley (11)

De Lucy Primary School, Abbey Wood

Little Weird Monster

'Hello, my name is Sir Gogle and I am the boss at the factory that makes eggs.'
Boom! 'Argh! Look, a black egg, it's hatching. Huh?'
A weird-looking monster came out.
'It does not look like a monster.'
'I think we should send it to the room of lava.'
'Boss, monsters come in different shapes and sizes.'
'Yes Jont, that's right.'
Ha ha ha! Little weird monster was very funny. One say little weird monster told Sir Gogle, 'I have to tell you something, I am going to start my own life.'
'I will miss you,' said Sir Gogle.

Leona Mustafaj (9)
De Lucy Primary School, Abbey Wood

The Mysterious Journey

The floor was ice cold. Missy was fighting for her strength but she couldn't go on any more. The next morning, she finally had enough strength to keep walking. Suddenly, she came across a strange-looking thing. It was a portal. Without thought, she went straight across it. *Bang!* Missy landed hard on her head.

'Hello,' whispered a voice.

Missy couldn't understand what it said so instead she said, 'Gloop gloop.'

After that very short conversation, they started playing with each other. As time went on, Missy learned English and now she was going to school and enjoying it.

Ella Nailubwama (10)

De Lucy Primary School, Abbey Wood

Being Berry Kind!

Carrissa, the violet-skinned creature, was strolling through the forest to select some berries. While she was wandering, she saw someone eat a poisonous berry. Trying to think of a way to help, she eventually came up with an idea. *That's it! An antidote!*

Grabbing all of the things that she could find, she mixed them altogether and carefully rubbed it on the monster's back, where the bruise was. The bruise eventually faded away and the monster thanked her for her help.

'How can I repay you?'

'You can tell me your name,' she replied.

'My name is Fraika.'

Leilah Dutton-Oxley (10)
De Lucy Primary School, Abbey Wood

Blaze's Army And Friends

Blaze was a fierce, powerful and plucky dragon that was red-skinned with orange-coloured wings and tummy. He didn't like his parents much even though they rarely saw each other. That all changed when his parents were alien-napped by the evil and ugly Zaptops. Blaze became angry like a flaming beast and called together a fighting hero team with friends: Blob, Bob, Jeff and Zaplight. Coming up with a devilishly amazing plan, they had full faith. They tricked the greedy Zaptops to eat an enormous sleeping potion-filled cake. Using his laser beams, Blaze cut through the cage and saved his parents.

Favour Omoregbee (10)
De Lucy Primary School, Abbey Wood

The Move To Lollipop-Land

New people in town can be hard, not for this creature. This creature is called Gum-drop. He moved to a place called Lollipop-land, he's never had a piece of candy in his life (funny that). Once he moved here, he found a lollipop.
'I wonder what this is?'
He picked up the lollipop, licked it and soon enough, went hyper. Gum-drop kept eating them. 'I'm aching!' he moaned, wanting more candy.
Opening his hand, what appeared was a... lollipop. Brilliant, he can make them appear, when he wants, wherever he wants. Lastly, he can make them appear at monster school.

Madison Bouchere (11)
De Lucy Primary School, Abbey Wood

The Misadventures of Wobbles (Part 1)

That is Wobbles. The hideous creature who never cares, and listen to this... he can turn into jelly in the middle of the night, twelve o'clock. It was a moonless, gloomy night and Wobbles was busy watching television. He was eating his crisps happily and heard a raucous sound in the kitchen. 'What was that?'

He had heard it near the fridge, so he looked inside and found... a bat! It flew into his face and at that very moment...

Ding, dong, ding, dong!

It was twelve o'clock and he transformed into jelly. He's gone... The bat had eaten him!

Melissa Farore (10)

De Lucy Primary School, Abbey Wood

Royal Alien Battle...

It was a normal day on Saturn. Arlia was just getting ready for her birthday party; being the princess of Saturn was really hard! All of a sudden, the ground started to shake uncontrollably. It was King Mars, Arlia's cousin, and soldiers.

'I am here to destroy your... princess, Arlia!' said King Mars in rage.

In the blink of an eye, King Mars' men started to conquer Saturn!

'Everyone, go and find shelter.'

Arlia could turn invisible, so she did, and flew to her cousin... When Arlia was angry, her tail charges and gives an electric shock.

Bang!

Damilola Oke (10)

De Lucy Primary School, Abbey Wood

Not Again Gnomton, Nom, Nom!

'I can't believe this!' says Grandpa Nom.
My own grandson ate all the Nom cookies without telling. This is a disgrace! What am I going to do? Nom 3, who was sitting next to the tree, just sat there listening to the dispute.
'We have to give cookies to Lord Special Nom! The Nom Nom of all time.'
As Grandpa sat down on the rocky road, Nom 3 said, 'We should do a harvest period so that we can restore cookies.'
'I think that's a good idea,' exclaimed Cinomton Nom.
So they decided to do that 'til the special day.

Ashley Kamina (10)
De Lucy Primary School, Abbey Wood

The Nerf Mission

One dark rainy night, Nerf Head got a letter through the post. The letter said...
Dear Nerf Head,
You are invited to complete a mission. The mission is to stop Master Scary Nerf shooting liquid at the babies. The liquid turns the babies invisible and they are causing trouble. If you can complete this mission you will become a hero.
Nerf Head accepted the mission and made his way to Jupiter using his RPG. When he landed on Jupiter he noticed Master Nerf. Nerf Head took out his net and captured the Mater, saving the babies and becoming a hero.

Bradley Osborne (11)
De Lucy Primary School, Abbey Wood

The Cyclops Mechanical Creature

Clopsian was waiting patiently for the Arodive to come. This was the day he had been waiting for. Finally, when the Arodive came, it took him two hours, thirty minutes to get to his homeland. The arrival was a very peculiar homecoming. Normally his friends and family would be crowding him. Suddenly, out of the shadows stepped Clopsian's enemy, Gogagagogogo. He was pale green and very exhausted. They started a battle. At the end, Clopsian used his energetic speed to outsmart his enemy. Clopsian won and his enemy never bothered him again. He lived happily thereafter.

Havivah Chinye (9)

De Lucy Primary School, Abbey Wood

Far Away And Alone

Once there was a pink, weird creature called Squishy and Squishy had a best friend called Squelch. Squelch was walking past a pond, Oreo was behind a bush. Squelch and Squishy ran into each other and they were talking about no one else being their friend. Oreo jumped out of the bush and said, 'How is my favourite friend called Squelch?'
Squishy was furious and he ran away. Wherever Squishy went, Oreo and Squelch were always there. Squishy had had enough so he moved to another land and another school. He found new friends and would always hang out.

Tomisin Halimah Olanrewaju (10)
De Lucy Primary School, Abbey Wood

Weird Life!

There's this lady monster thing that lived in Spatula Land, her name is Misorobotface. She is very good at growing armpit hair and giving scary, jump scare surprises and she doesn't like people that don't hold spatulas.

Later that day, she saw a man that wasn't holding a spatula and he was in Spatula Land, so she got mad and walked up to the man and asked him, 'Why are you here?'

He was speechless then she kicked him out, so he ran away crying and started killing people. So the police arrested him forever and ever for murdering people.

Emi Llukovi
De Lucy Primary School, Abbey Wood

The Haunted School

The Alipire was in the school hiding in the playground when the children went outside, the Alipire jumped out of hiding and got thirty kids, took them to the school hall and enjoyed their blood. The teachers found out that the Alipire sucked thirty kids' blood. They called the good aliens so they could destroy the Alipire but he was too strong, so the teachers called more good aliens to come. They destroyed Alipire and they put blood back into the thirty kids, but they didn't notice that another Alipire was on Earth! The disease spread and spread until death!

Samuel Fayoyin (7)
De Lucy Primary School, Abbey Wood

The Tales Of Naruto Uzumaki

Naruto went to a meeting but out of nowhere, five enemies attacked and declared war. Naruto was getting ready for war. They ambushed the villains and managed to destroy three of them. Suddenly, a god was summoned. Finally Naruto transformed into god-mode, but it wasn't enough. Out of nowhere, Saskay came and helped demolish the villains. It was a piece of cake. Suddenly, the boss came so Naruto and Sakay summed a 9-tail. Eventually they won the impossible. They didn't know how to defeat Boruto, so the heroes used an ancient summon that defeated Boruto.

Jameel Mousavi (11)
De Lucy Primary School, Abbey Wood

The Mechanical Coincidence

One day, near a village on an unknown island, there was a smart but lonely scientist who at least wanted a friend. At an awkward moment later, the lonely person had a brilliant idea! He got to work and made a creature called Dominator. He was a robot dragon with many designs. The next day, an angry mob came. They thought Dominator was a monster even though he was gentle, but can be rough. They charged but then there was a rumble; everyone escaped the island before... the volcano erupted! Dominator's friend left and the dragon was left alone, unsafe...

Junior Anderson (10)
De Lucy Primary School, Abbey Wood

Woddles And The Space Bird

One stormy night on Planet Mars, Woddles, the nine-eared, spotty monster was suddenly whisked away by a spaghetti tornado. Woddles opened his gangly eyes, but was alone in the darkness. Luckily, his nine solar-powered ears were fully charged, so that he could listen out for his free ride back to Mars. Suddenly, Woddles heard a loud squeak, followed by an almighty crash. His mechanical ears steered him towards the bushes... He carefully, climbed aboard the bird's scaly back and grabbed its fluffy horns, before it took flight back to his home on Mars!

James Thomas Eaton (9)
De Lucy Primary School, Abbey Wood

The Monster Boys

Once upon a time there was a boy and his friend. They became monsters with lots of eyes every night and became enemies. Night after night, with their blue arms and googly eyes, they would fight each other. To sneak up on each other, they would camouflage. When the sun rose, everything would change back to normal. All the mess they made by stomping on everything would clear up and they'd become friends. Every night was the same, with all the building reappearing, and the two friends would turn from enemies to friends all day long.

Ayesha Rauf (9)
De Lucy Primary School, Abbey Wood

Smuky Lucky Nupy Emily Adventure

Once upon a time there was a crazy, little creature called Smuky Lucky Nupy Emily. For all her life she had always lived in Australia. But when she wanted to go to school, well she didn't know that she couldn't go to school. So there was a crazy creature school. She didn't make any friends. Maybe because she didn't fit in. Everyone made her upset and it wasn't a good place to go. So she just did home school. She loved it because she made friends across the street. She loved school and she would never get bullied again.

Mariam Oladejo (9)
De Lucy Primary School, Abbey Wood

Disaster

One day, there was a monster. He was sad but a little dragon came and was lonely and the monster asked the dragon if the dragon could be the monster's friend.

The dragon said, 'Yes but my friends told me that I had to go to a castle and attack.'

But the dragon did not want to and the monster said, 'Don't worry, I'll come with you.'

But the dragon said, 'It is too dangerous because the knights will try to kill you!'

But the monster went and got killed and the dragon was sad and kept on crying.

Harry Brown (8)
De Lucy Primary School, Abbey Wood

Harry Mr Barry Destroys Doodle Noodle

Harry Mr Barry came out and saw that his neighbourhood had noodles everywhere. Then he knew who was being very noodly; it was Doodle Noodle, the evilest villain in the world! He knew where to find him. Well, there was no time to waste! Doodle Noodle had gone to the terrible noodle shop in the entire Monstymous Castocous, and that's where he lives and hides out. Then Harry Mr Barry went in and saw he had shot noodles everywhere. So Harry Mr Barry punched Doodle Noodle and he shot himself with noodles and both exploded.

Misheal Prince Okorogu (8)
De Lucy Primary School, Abbey Wood

The Clever Crystal Won Again

Many hundreds of years ago, Crystal walked in a deep, dark forest with her friend called Lily, she's a fox. They walked through the spooky forest, looking for their prey. Crystal and Lily saw a squirrel moving around, looking for a nut to eat in the tree. Crystal and Lily chased the squirrel to the tree. Crystal hit Lily because of the squirrel. Lily punched Crystal on the eye. Crystal pushed Lily onto the floor, and the squirrel fell off the tree. Lily scratched Crystal on her body. Crystal saw a squirrel and caught it. Both of them ate it.

Ishika Anil Patel (10)
De Lucy Primary School, Abbey Wood

The War Of The Two Galaxies

Draigon was training to fight because something from the Iron Galaxy was coming. Once, the training place was closed and Draigon found it strange. *Boom*, there was a flash of lightning. 'Oh no, he's coming,' said Draigon. Each day it got worse and one day, it got so bad that Draigon knew he was going to see the monster. Monster came, but Draigon had an army and with a big bam, they were all fighting. Draigon cut through the monster, the laser beam touched its heart and it was dead. From that day, Draigon was a true hero.

Kanishk Aggarwal (7)
De Lucy Primary School, Abbey Wood

The Messiest Monster

My character is called The Messiest Monster and he was as messy as everyone. Nobody liked him. Nobody liked him because he could kill people easily. Also he lived in London, that is why as well. The Messiest Monster ever could hurt anyone. He had spikes to kill you if you touched it. Also, when smoke came out, you could not breathe when he growled. He had twenty legs come out because that is how angry he got. He got his temper by getting stressed or annoyed by other people making him. The Messiest Monster had warts that were poisonous.

Evie Shepherd (9)
De Lucy Primary School, Abbey Wood

The Monster Hole

Once, there was a snake-like figure called Stuart. He was from Zombieville, He lived with his creepy family. One day, he went on an adventure to a jungle. When he arrived, he explored and found a hole. He dropped a pebble down there and he didn't hear it hit the bottom. He was freaked out and heard another monster. Stuart said, 'Hello.' There was no answer. Stuart was scared, so scared that he pulled his razor-sharp spines out. The hole was dark and gloomy, it was scary. Suddenly, it jumped out and pushed Stuart. He fell down!

Harley Dowling (10)
De Lucy Primary School, Abbey Wood

Bob The Crazy Monster

A hairy, scruffy and bulky monster called Bob, who lived up in the scary mountains of Hairy-Ville with his three brothers; Bert, Trash and Nigel. Until the day he ran away to Crazy-Ville because everyone said he was too hairy. Everyone he met was extremely crazy. He missed his brothers, so he would return to the valleys and very soon, he went to a creative owl and asked for a quirky haircut so he could return to his family. Everyone loved his new style and everyone copied his fashionable look. Bob was the happiest monster in Hairy-Ville.

Rochelle Sheehan (11)
De Lucy Primary School, Abbey Wood

Alien Vs Predators: The Hunted

There was a very strange creature lurking in the research facility. No man could go alone. But one day, the alien tricked the soldiers and predators. The soldiers put their military base on lockdown. It took too long and they were in. The aliens knocked them out and gone too were the predators. This was a real fight, the predators slashed, struck at the alien. Some died, some survived. The alien won the fight. They got smarter until they built a bigger base, it was huge. The place was Death Valley. The name of the city was Alien Empire.

Jose McGure (10)
De Lucy Primary School, Abbey Wood

DeathX

Once upon a space time there was a team of three monsters called DeathX, Deathman and Inferno. They were all on their way to destroy Earth. After one year, it was just space and they were the only ones alive and then DeathX and his team built a new planet and they were the three kings. DeathX made a million mummy slaves and they lived together in an alien palace. Then another alien came to their team which had gravity power and his name was Gravinsion and he was DeathX's older brother who'd survived. The aliens lived happily.

Faaz Akram Khan (9)

De Lucy Primary School, Abbey Wood

The Monster Who Had A Roarsome Friend

Once upon a time there lived a pretty, flying, gentle, invisible monster called Lilly. She was very nice. Everyone hated her, she was too nice. She needed help to be mean, but she couldn't. She tried to prank with a whoopee pillow, but to say sorry she baked a pie. They were friends. She tried to put whipped cream in the queen of Monsetring Town, but said sorry by making cupcakes. She could not believe she couldn't be horrible. She was so sad. A monster came and said to her, 'Just be yourself.' They became friends forever.

Precious-Nicole Kamsiyiochukwu Odiaka (7)
De Lucy Primary School, Abbey Wood

Grimer's Crazy Epic Story

One stormy night, a nine-year-old boy was in his house, where his mum would have been shopping, but she is in a wheelchair. She got hit, but enough about that... He works for a secret agency, Workout, and he had awesome battle skills. But one odd night, he kept hearing noises from an inch away, so he moved his blind then *boom!* There were creatures, OMG! But not for Grimer, he was so cool he could kill them all. *Boom! Bang! Blast!* But they were trying to help so they shook hands and lived.

Tyler David O'Sullivan (9)
De Lucy Primary School, Abbey Wood

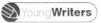

The Mystery Of The Spiky Slug Monster

There was a mysterious hill rising from the ground. Out popped a tiny, but fierce, monster. His name was Spiky Slug Monster and he was the first monster seen. One day, he crept up on a little child and leapt onto his back. The child screamed and called the police. The police took the monster away but it escaped from the car. The police were suspicious at what happened. They didn't know that he had magic tricks and knew how to escape. Police were spread far and wide. The police were more suspicious than ever. He was in a tree.

Klaudia Valero (8)
De Lucy Primary School, Abbey Wood

Untitled

Jason was clown hunting at night with his friends and he came across a wolf, they ran for their lives and they found a cabin. But they didn't know that it said: *Do Not Enter*. They slept there for a night and there were weird noises that were creaking. Jason woke up and a clown appeared. He was worried. Jason got a plank of wood and smashed it across the clown's huge head. His friends woke up and started to attack the clown with Jason. RIP clown. The clown died because they chucked him off of the roof.

Jayden Argent (10)
De Lucy Primary School, Abbey Wood

Your Worst Nightmare

Benson is a bad ghost. He can see through the past and present. One of his eyes was red so he could see through the future. Benson lives in space. He can breathe in space. Benson looks into the future and finds out the humans are coming. Benson gets into a fight. Benson turns into a ball while the humans are standing still like bowling pins. Benson rolls into them and knocks them over. The humans cry and start to leave. The humans say that they won't come to that planet ever again. Benson agreed with them and they promised.

Joshua Conweh (9)
De Lucy Primary School, Abbey Wood

Untitled

After fighting for so long, he was tried. Ruby's polearm dropped on the Earth's ground. The second gem war was reminding him of the first war when his diamond, pink diamond was... broken. Thinking of this, tears filled his eyes but he didn't even realised a crazy Lace Agate and a Biggs Jasper were spin-dashing at him. Before they could reach him, Ruby heard a song and everyone was running, but it was too late. He was cursed by the diamonds! His monster form was ugly, roaming around for thousands of years on Earth!

Yannick Pandam (10)
De Lucy Primary School, Abbey Wood

Old World

It was a lovely morning in Kangton Town and Amelia felt like going to explore her town. She went outside to see a tunnel under her house. It went so low down, almost to the middle of Earth. She went down the tunnel to explore, this place looked like the place her mum lived! The place was colourful. It was like a world full of rainbow. Her mum said it would be called Old World and it had a tag that said: 'This place will be getting broken down and filled with rainbow mud'. So Amelia just let it go.

Debbie Ogunade (9)
De Lucy Primary School, Abbey Wood

Planet Shape-Shift

One day on planet Shape-Shift, Daisy was relaxing when *bang!* There was a massive crash, so she decided to go check out where the crash was. She set off until she came across some grey falcons planning how they were going to blow up and destroy planet Shape-Shift. So Daisy shape-shifted into a dog and attacked the falcons and got some friends to pitch in and help. The falcons were very naughty and conniving, so the slugs and dogs convinced the falcons to stop and to be very good and to stop being naughty.

Lacey Lilly Scerri (9)
De Lucy Primary School, Abbey Wood

The Warted Monster

Once upon a time there lived a monster with moon rock powers. He went into town and there he was, face-to-face with Cheer Pom and Glass It All. Cheer Pom threw her poms at Warty but Warty used his wart powers, then it hit Cheer Pom. He hit Glass It All, then Glass It All was still standing. Then Warty aimed at his arms then *boom!* Glass It All broke. Then to celebrate, Warty went for cake but then Glass It All came back, then Warty was fighting. Then he hit Glass It All, then he was dead.

Kennedy Marie Tyler (9)
De Lucy Primary School, Abbey Wood

Courageous Corey The Alien!

In the depths of Planet Pop, there was an alien that could fly. She loved to show her extreme, wonderful talents. By the chocolate lake, a putrid, evil villain laughed dramatically at Corey. Immediately, she had burst into tears. Then India was nicer to Corey. One early morning, India did a majestic, shimmering spell to put on Corey to take her powers away. Corey had a sister, Skye. She had known about India, the villain. Corey and Skye went to a dangerous war. India lost and Corey thanked Skye. Corey was famous on Pop.

Natalie Osaremi Egbe (9)
De Lucy Primary School, Abbey Wood

The Strange Doctor

Once, there was a creature and his name was Doctor Strange. He had eight eyes and he could look at every direction without turning! He was 100% friendly but was only a doctor for other creatures. But the only thing was, no other creature liked him because he was a nerd! There there, now don't tell anyone because it is a VIP secret! Doctor Strange has always wanted to be a doctor, but now he does not want to have this job any more because, well, let's stop this because he is going to give me bad dreams!

Maddison Mitchell (9)
De Lucy Primary School, Abbey Wood

The Greedy Monster

Once, there was a greedy monster who was hunting for food like small monsters. One day, he saw a mouse in the jungle.
'What are you doing little mouse, hmmm?'
'I want to cross this river.'
'OK, climb on my back,' said the monster, 'Ow! Climb on my head. Ow! Climb on my nose.' Suddenly he tossed him up, up in the sky and gobbled him in one bite! He was the meanest, baddest and the greediest monster in the world. He takes your food and kills you but somebody killed him!

Esther Omonijo Tiamiyu (7)
De Lucy Primary School, Abbey Wood

Mercury Monster Munchkin

Mercury Monster came in to meet his mum with his stinky body. His mum asked him to go to the shop with his laser beam eyes to go and get skrill pudding. Mercury got shopping bags and went shopping. When he got there, the door was locked. He turned invisible to get in. He looked around. There wasn't skrill pudding. So he ran back home and told his mum there was no skrill pudding. His mum had to go and check if there wasn't any pudding. There was none, but there was skrill bread so they munched it all up.

Jedediah Onokpasa (8)
De Lucy Primary School, Abbey Wood

Blobstar The Great

Blobstar trudged through the path to the stadium. He had to win one of the contests there, otherwise he wouldn't be able to get home. He lived on the Ugly Islands of Uranus, where he was free. Right now, he was on Earth and felt like he was in prison. He was good at dance but every time he did a dance contest, he lost to one person or another. But this contest, he felt more determined to win. Soon, the contest started. Blobstar was not doing so well, but he didn't give up and ended up winning! Finally home!

Theresa Awoleke (11)
De Lucy Primary School, Abbey Wood

The Boy That Picked Up This Yummy Sweet

Once upon a time there was a boy that was going to school and found a sweet on the floor. He picked it up, opened it and ate it all. But then he suddenly turned into a horrible and scary monster. When he went into class, everyone was frightened. They were scared and ran away into another room. But when he went into the boy's bathroom, he saw his face and was terrified. He saw that he had green, fuzzy hair and was blue. After a while, he had learnt his lesson not to pick things from the floor.

Sabiha Haque (9)
De Lucy Primary School, Abbey Wood

Friends Forever After

Lightning Speed was running very fast. It was getting hot so he went to the blood cafe. He used the holes in his shiny, sharp daggers. Then he set off to running again. He was running and running and he still was not tired until he was lost. He thought, then he had an idea. He decided to dig and use his hyper sonic detector, on his hands. He did get lost until someone came. They spoke and they were best friends. They spoke for an hour, now they know each other so Lightning Speed got out. Friends forever.

Michael Daniel (8)
De Lucy Primary School, Abbey Wood

Slimetug's Hungry Day

In the beginning, there was an alien called Slimetug and he had just come back from a long walk and he was very hungry after he'd come back from the very long walk. Then he saw a different alien that was eating a lot of food. He was over the moon, he wanted to eat it but he was not allowed so they had a fight and they were very upset and sad for them, so they said sorry and apologised and then they were friends. So they shared the food and they were happy. After, they lived happily again.

Iyegbekosa Bezaleel Edo-Osagie (10)
De Lucy Primary School, Abbey Wood

Red Nose Heart, Friends, Mum And Dad And Family

In a planet far away, two weeks ago, Red Nose Heart met her friends on planet Blob. When she got there, she met Sarha, Natalie, Jemima and Jessica. They went back to Planet Flowers, and then they went to the beach on Planet Bobble, right next to them. After they finished at the beach, they decided to get some food and go to the park then they went to the funfair. They bought candyfloss, lollies, cakes, more cakes, more candyfloss and more lollipops. They caught a duck and got a prize, it was a fish!

Maddie-Lee Reader-Penfold (9)
De Lucy Primary School, Abbey Wood

Fire Boy

One day, there was a creature called Fire Boy. He was a nice boy, he had no enemies. He had wings, horns, fangs. He was a dragon. He was stumbling through the forest, just strolling through the forest, playing with his friend called Cozzy. They were playing football and they fell on the floor. There was an invisible split screen, they saw a puzzle. They had to solve it. It looked very hard but they had to do it, so they got on with it. They had to put the shapes in the right place. They did it all!

Aaron Ellery (9)
De Lucy Primary School, Abbey Wood

The Universe Is In The Aliens' Hands

It's been thousands of years since the aliens conquered the universe. Until then, the massive Masnones came to destroy the planets but there was one alien that was kind and generous. His name was Monster Jeff. He was the kindest alien on the planet. There was a problem, the aliens were coming onto the planets fast, so Monster Jeff tried stopping them to get off the planet. He moved a massive UFO and it worked! They didn't come onto the planet. Monster Jeff was proud of what he'd done.

Maddie Louise Darby (11)
De Lucy Primary School, Abbey Wood

The Codo Creature

One day there was a creature called Codo and he was afraid of humans because they wanted to kill him. He was really scared and his long tongue was shivering because of them. Codo did not know what to do, so he went away and tried to go somewhere where no humans were. Then suddenly, he found a pretty, fluffy coat on the floor and wore it so he looked like a human and the humans would think that he was not a creature. Then Codo walked past the humans and they did not realise that it was Codo.

Amelisa Mucaj (10)
De Lucy Primary School, Abbey Wood

A Crazy Creature Called Geek

There lived a crazy creature called Geek. He was so hairy and he had five eyes. Also he had big, big fangs. He also had an awesome power to turn people into ice! His enemy was called Ice Master. Then he was walking, until he saw Ice Master. Geek got his ice gun and shot, but he missed. After, he distracted him and he got him! But he had a healing potion. So Geek shot him five times and he was dead forever now. Then everyone was cheering because he saved the day! After that he never came again.

Joel Adjei Twum (7)
De Lucy Primary School, Abbey Wood

Brutra And Eagla

Once upon a time there lived a starfish called Brutra. He lived on a stinky beach. His horrible habit was sucking blood. Brutra had an enemy called Eagla, he liked sucking blood too. How Brutra sucks blood is when an animal comes by, he pounces up and bites it with its snake-like fangs and he has venom. Eagla digs himself in sand and when an animal comes close, they both found their meal. When they saw each other, they fought and fought until the seagull went away...

Aaron Kamina (8)
De Lucy Primary School, Abbey Wood

The Adventures Of Cooka-Ladooka!

In the dark, deep area, Cooka-ladooka was ready for an adventure, so he got ready to jump and sprang up into the air like a rocket shooting up into the sky! Suddenly, he landed somewhere that he had never been before. It was a pool party, so he jumped in. As soon as he got there, he was scared. He jumped again to a different place. It was a park. He got scared because there were lots and lots of kids looking at him, so he jumped off to another place again, but he was back at home!

Victoria Oluwasemilore Abdul (10)
De Lucy Primary School, Abbey Wood

Untitled

In the castle, Natiania was thinking now to known as a hero, not a princess. You know why? Because tomorrow was prom and she wanted to be thanked. Then when she was walking, she heard a big *bang!* It was a gigantic bird. It started shooting lasers at her. She managed to duck and attacked him with lasers. He fell down and down into the deep ends of the canyon. When she went home, she was awarded with a medal and a trophy. She was not just a princess, she was a knight!

Davina Olukoko (10)
De Lucy Primary School, Abbey Wood

The Mean Bullies

There was a boy called Kice and he was getting bullied by some people called Red Noshear, Wobbles and Hearty Bear. One day, he went to a lesson for ninja moves and he would never stop until he got his moves right for the bullies that bullied him. He was going to get them back one day. He saw the bullies, he didn't know what to do, he used his moves on them and everyone was scared of him. One day, he saw Wobbles and he knocked her out and she was scared of him forever.

Tyler Jerome Newman (10)
De Lucy Primary School, Abbey Wood

PooBrain Gets Bullied

One day, there was a monster called PooBrain. He had a body made out of poo and his eyes were on his wing. He went to a school named Monster Sky and he comes from the sky. PooBrain gets bullied in school by Golddigger and Sharkface and always gets upset when he goes home, but one day he gets stronger and never gives up. He goes and tells the bullies to stop what they are doing to other monsters. Then PooBrain beats up the bullies and the bullies never get seen again.

Damilola Mosuro (10)
De Lucy Primary School, Abbey Wood

Plankton's Saga

Plankton ran along on his bottom half, while he was looking for a shelter, when he came across a friend. He and his friend got stuck together. They had a big mouth and strong suction, they got along well together. When they went to Slobber School, the creature learned how to be crazy. Plankton wasn't a normal creature, neither was the other slug. They also had big horns on their heads instead of ears. The horns were as big as a bull's horns - bigger than my own ears!

Rubie Nicole Worf (8)
De Lucy Primary School, Abbey Wood

Tikka And The Lumber Jack Tree

Tikka, a miniscule red pom-pom monster, was stranded in the Crazy Forest! It was all because of Tootsie, Tikka's enemy. She always tried to mess with her or get her in trouble. She looked around and saw a Lumber Jack tree! A wishing tree! Whatever you wished would come true. But only for a week. Tikka thought very carefully. Finally; it hit her.

'I wish that Tootsie got bullied.'

A spark flew from the tree and exploded. That means the wish came true.

Chiamaka Udochuku Obosi (11)

De Lucy Primary School, Abbey Wood

Save The Planet

TeethyMcLoveFace leapt across the lava on Loveland. Then she let a lovebird go.
'Oh no!' she shouted, 'StarryShine moved. Also my bird got eaten by a lion!'
StarryShine jumped onto a skyscraper. TeethyMcLoveFace flew up the skyscraper to StarryShine although it collapsed. She grasped onto a window ledge while pulling herself in, yelling, 'Run down the stairs and save yourself because I'll save Loveland.'
She ran up the stairs to the roof.
'What are you doing?' she bellowed, 'This is not your land so go away!'
StarryShine ran as fast as she could. Teethy got a cape. She fixed Loveland.

Lizzie Herelle-Savage (8)
Henwick Primary School, Eltham

Moppy McTentical And The Rocks

As Moppy slowly cleaned the floor, some children were throwing rocks behind him. Suddenly, all the children threw the rocks at once and they all landed on Moppy's tentacles.

'Ouch!' whimpered Moppy.

Seconds, minutes, hours, days and weeks went past. Just then, Moppy heard a noise. It was his friend, Vacuma.

'I can help you!' exclaimed Vacuma.

So she lifted up the rocks and Moppy was free!

'Thank you!' cried Moppy.

Happily, Moppy and Vacuma carried on cleaning. A few minutes later, there was a turn for the unexpected. Vacuma went missing! Moppy found out that the rocks were magic.

Melanie Stoyanova (8)
Henwick Primary School, Eltham

Eteon's Birthday Surprise!

One morning, Eteon awoke to a strange sound. It was his neighbours, John and Jilly, they were jelly monsters.
'Uh, what are they doing now?' Eteon shouted.
'Oh, we're just making worm cakes in the noisy oven again,' giggled John and Jilly.
'They're for you,' they laughed.
But Eteon was still sleeping! When he woke up, he went downstairs but it was too dark for him to see so he turned on the lights.
'Happy birthday Eteon,' John and Jilly shouted.
Eteon was speechless, he was even crying because it was so amazing.
'Thank you, this is the best!'

Viktoria Marinusovna Broeren (8)
Henwick Primary School, Eltham

The Day Pingo Got Lost In A School!

One starry night, Pingo woke up from some sort of shouting. It was his little brother, Bixxy.

'Hey Pingo,' shouted Bixxy, 'I thought last night you said that we were going to explore Earth.'

'Yes, but I said at midnight and that is in five minutes,' Pingo said tiredly.

'But we need to get ready,' explained Bixxy.

'OK then, let's get ready,' said Pingo.

They got ready and left for Earth. When they got to Earth, they landed on a school. Sadly, they got very lost! Luckily, Pingo's friends helped and they got Pingo back home to his planet, Pinland!

Theadora Burke (8)

Henwick Primary School, Eltham

The Adventure

Siley, the scared yeti, walked along a spooky cave with his long, sticky tongue when he suddenly saw a glow. Siley went near the light slowly. It was so bright that Siley's eyes nearly went blind. He went inside the glow and he went 2000 years back, when the dinosaurs lived.

He said, 'Where am I?' and started walking when a dinosaur started chasing him.

Siley said, 'Someone help!'

He saw a teleporter and went inside it. He went back to 2017 but his house was gone! He went to find his house but he couldn't find it.

Ismail Cemil Ustundag (8)

Henwick Primary School, Eltham

The Monster Who Lived In The Forest

Bogurt was a friendly creature who could sometimes be mischievous. He was a shape-shifter who used his skills to play tricks on his friends. He was a middle-sized giant. He called his friends, Bobby the Bogurt, Lolly Bogurt and Holly the Bogurt. He was a friendly creature, who loved tricks. He loved tricks and hide-and-seek and he was a famous creature in town. Everyone loved his jokes, the other creatures laughed and had so much fun. Every day everyone played. He went to visit his friend, he looked around then said, 'I'm going home.'

Maddie Foley (8)
Henwick Primary School, Eltham

The Evil Rabbit

Once upon a time there was a girl and she was all alone, then she went to the garden and she saw a creepy rabbit and the rabbit's name was Fluffy. Fluffy was scared of the girl and the girl wanted to keep the creature as a pet. The girl took the creature on a walk and they found a hole and there were rabbits. The creature killed the rabbits with his laser hands. Then they went home and they had lots of fun. Fluffy killed the girl's cat, and so Fluffy never had a lovely home.

Yezda Demirkol (8)
Henwick Primary School, Eltham

My Creature

Once upon a time there lived a creature that was called Billy. Billy had lots of friends and only one enemy. He was trained by a girl called Lucy. She was very nice and kind. He was very colourful, smelly and he had lots of tricks and magic. They both lived in Greenland, where mostly monsters lived with their owners. They used to eat bones, green soup and smelly stuff from the bin. *Yum, tasty!* But Lucy said, 'Gross! I have some cereal to eat.'

Mia Vuckovic (9)
Henwick Primary School, Eltham

Zappre

Once upon a time there was a kid called Astro, he was a very gentle and intelligent boy that liked to work and had a father and mother. Then his mother got hit and disappeared. Astro wanted to know how to get her back, she gave him a crystal to find her. He had a great adventure which gave him zapping powers to zap people. He was called Zapper. He stopped at a place and Man Goat was there, his mom's old enemy. He tried to defeat him; and at last, he did! The world saver!

Jesse Ku (9)
Henwick Primary School, Eltham

My Crazy Monster

One early morning, Bibideybob packed up his suitcase getting ready to fly away on holiday in his spaceship. He was going to Monster City to find new friends. He was waking up to go to university in the morning. He found the work hard. When they got a break, he tried finding friends. He saw one bot and they played football games together, they had fun. But the next day, he had to go back home to his family. He asked his new friends to come back with him. They said yes - a happy ending!

Sonny Godbolt (9)
Henwick Primary School, Eltham

The Lonely Monster

Once upon a time there was a monster with green hair and pink skin. She was all alone on Wackat and had nobody to play with. One day, she found a clone machine and made a clone. She named her Pink. Then she made another clone and named her Blue. She was relieved that she finally had some friends to play with. Then all of them made a city that took one year to build. The people of the city named her Elizabeth and her happy nickname was Joyful. And they lived happily ever after.

Nevaeh Conteh (9)
Henwick Primary School, Eltham

Scary Slug Face

The bottom of the garden is an eerie place, because there lives a monster named Scary Slug Face. He usually lives on Mercury, but he comes down to Earth to eat the grass. Don't get too close or he might dissolve into acid! Mr Scary Slug Face had been found in someone's garden and they tried to pick him up, but suddenly he dissolved in defence. Scary Slug Face almost burned her fingers off and he was never seen again!

Bobby Patrick George Tolley (8)
Henwick Primary School, Eltham

Sythe

In a cave, in the Rockies, a preposterous little creature slept, snoring loudly. Then there was a loud crash and a brave man, Steven appeared in the pitch-black cave.
'Well, well, well, what d' we 'ave 'ere then?' boomed a deep voice.
Scared, terrified, shocked, Sythe opened his mouth and said, sounding tougher than before, 'M' name's Sythe and you're messing with the wrong monster.'
Steven fired a bullet but Sythe quickly dodged it and grabbed him with his claw and flung him out of the cave.
'This won't be the last of me!' Steve shouted.
'Y' sure?' Sythe shouted...

Sebastian Recordon (8)
St Anselm's Catholic Primary School, Wandsworth

Oojimuflip

Oojimuflip, a 24-eyed alien with an Afro and turquoise skin, was fighting for his star system with his friends. He was rather large. You would have thought the intergalactic robber team would be freaked out by such a creature, but they had encountered strangers before. The intergalactic team had sophisticated weapons. Unfortunately, Oojimuflip and his friends only had custard pies. The intergalactic team were hardened warriors. Unfortunately, Oojimuflip and his friends just wanted to lounge about. However, Oojimuflip had a secret weapon and decided it was time to deploy it. It was a poisonous fart! This would save them all.

Benjamin Wevill (8)
St Anselm's Catholic Primary School, Wandsworth

A Close Call For Lollylol!

One beautiful, bright, sunny day, Lollylol went outside to earn some money by performing backflips. Suddenly, a gigantic, evil-looking, blood-red bird swooped down and grasped Lollylol in its razor-sharp, glowing, yellow beak. Luckily, Lollylol had been practising her superpower, shooting pink slime traps from her hairbow's mouth, so she shot one straight at the bird and they dramatically fell to the ground. Lollylol's poor heart was beating faster and faster as she was not sure if her worst nightmare was still alive. From that moment on, she never dared in her whole entire life to leave her beloved home again.

Ella Lewis (8)
St Anselm's Catholic Primary School, Wandsworth

The Monster Who Stopped The War

Doda finally woke up from being unconscious. He looked around and suddenly shouted, 'This isn't home.'

He looked around some more and realised he was in Chinganut and there was a war happening there! There were sounds of gunshots and soldiers were rushing in every second, in need of emergency help. Doda knew he had to do something, but he didn't know what. Suddenly, an idea popped up in his mind... He would go into the middle of the battlefield and say to everyone, 'Why are you fighting? You're part of the same country.' Then slowly, everyone became friends forever.

Gianluca Pietro Acanfora (9)
St Anselm's Catholic Primary School, Wandsworth

Let's Do This!

Once, on a hill, Stupideo lived in a house, sorry, an amazing house, and all he could do was sit and eat but at least there were fun things to do. One day, he was eating fruit and all of a sudden, his enemies bashed in.

'Now that hurt!' said one of them.

'This place is mine and I want it back,' exclaimed Plonkton.

'Well, how're you going to get it?' said Stupideo.

'By fighting,' said Plonkton.

'OK, let's do this!'

Pow! Punch! Ouch! So sore.

'Wooooo, see I won.'

He sat there every day, even now.

Victoria Alexandra Pajaczkowska (9)
St Anselm's Catholic Primary School, Wandsworth

Zibadong's Lake

Zibadong stood in front of a mysterious silhouette in an ebony hoody. The strange figure was almost identical to the unknown creature that had come to her, while she was sharpening her razor-edged body spikes, to instruct her to come to this dark, gloomy place. Finally, Zibadong took a humongous breath of courage and nervously said, 'Who are you?'

A gust of wind blew back his hood to reveal the snake-like features of Lazoom. Zibadong could see starving, slimy leeches in the 1000-feet lake. Suddenly, Zibadong realised Lazoom's plan. Zibadong let out a shrill, horrified cry...

Ruby Cox (9)
St Anselm's Catholic Primary School, Wandsworth

Zinky's Troubles

Bang! With a gigantic thud, Zinky arrived on Earth...

Why am I here on Earth, not Mars? he pondered. All of a sudden, there was a van, with a human inside. That was the moment that he remembered that his enemies: birds, dogs, cats and humans lived on Earth.

'Oh no, I need to go home,' Zinky screamed.

He was too late, the man in the van got out and made his way to Zinky stating, 'You! You can't be here! You will dissolve within six hours - you need to get home!' exclaimed the man fretfully.

Zinky was trembling.

Niamh Worrell (9)
St Anselm's Catholic Primary School, Wandsworth

Far From Home

Lazerblonk had found himself staring at his best friend, Ricoh. They had travelled far from their home planet and were angry at each other. As well as this, their ship was instantly doomed so they couldn't get back to their planet, Zigzag. How awful was the sight on their faces? They couldn't get back home to where they lived. They had to stay there forever! Suddenly, they heard a zig from Zigzag!

'Zigzag is near, Ricoh! I can see it with my own eyes!'

'It's true, I can see it!' Lazerblonk shouted excitedly, thinking he was going to explode. Wow!

Elizabeth Ilona Anghenica (9)

St Anselm's Catholic Primary School, Wandsworth

The Final Battle

The Coros trampled forward with his eyes beaming at the crown jewel. He was thinking could his two repulsive legs get past the guards? He touched one of the guards and roared to one of the guards, 'Balthazar wants his crown.'

The guard nodded. Coros ran away and became himself again. Balthazar saw him out of the corner of his eye. He elbowed him with a snarl on his face. He dropped the crown and was about to fall over. Balthazar declared, 'This is the end of you!'

The Mallaper saved him and pushed Balthazar and waddled away into heaven.

Joseph Awad (9)
St Anselm's Catholic Primary School, Wandsworth

The Eye Monster

Ericsson, the eye monster, had gleaming, piercing eyes, as white as snow. His circular, green wart, oozed out electricity. This helped him to attract the iPods and iPhones to his body! His eight eyes swayed ferociously through the wind, as they looked for their next victim! One bright morning, he made his way to Wittering Road. Feeling rather ravenous, he cautiously made his way to the houses and tasted his first iPhone. After devouring his 100th gadget, he heard sounds of very frightened, terrified and annoyed children. Like a shot, he flew away and went back to Eye Land.

Maria Ikpase (8)
St Anselm's Catholic Primary School, Wandsworth

The Curious Case Of Belly Button

Have you ever had a feel around in your belly button and picked out a piece of fluff? Well, I'm here to tell you how mine got in. I have a creature named Heso. He found a little bit of fluff for his pillow, then he was looking for somewhere warm and dark to sleep. First, he tried the fridge, without the light on.

'Too cold,' Heso grumbled.

Next, he found an open tub and went in.

He then exclaimed, 'Too light.'

As a last resort, he went into my belly button and laid down his pillow.

Heso whispered, 'Perfect!'

Riley Jein (8)

St Anselm's Catholic Primary School, Wandsworth

Bongo Vs Zintopia

One Sunday, when fog hung over the sky like a blanket, Bongo, a three-eyed monster with a toxic gas horn and fire powers, was strolling home from his long day of hunting. Suddenly, he heard some rustling in a nearby bush! Some gnarled nails dig into Bongo's leg, leaving him badly bleeding. Bongo then identified his attacker: his enemy, Zintopia! He realised that he must used his powers and released some toxic gas and scalded Zintopia with fire. He fell to his knees and surrendered. Bongo made his way home and arrived just in time for dinner, home-made lasagne!

Gene Allaway (9)
St Anselm's Catholic Primary School, Wandsworth

The Near Attack

Suddenly, Zantok heard a noise. It sounded like someone hitting rock with a pick-axe. Then he heard whispers and almost immediately he knew what was there. It was a human! He got ready to strike and flew quite close to where the sound was coming from. Then from where the sound was, some stone cracked open and out came two humans. Zantok then used all his skills and they almost instantly noticed. They then got out their pick-axes and pointed them at him. Zantok then slithered at them extremely quickly, but then the second human screamed and Zantok stopped.

Rafael Das (9)
St Anselm's Catholic Primary School, Wandsworth

Aqua The Mermaid

A tingling sensation ran quickly from my knees and ankles then feet. I felt nervous, wondering what was going on. I felt strange like never before. Someone or something was tickling me, like a brush scraping off my strange-feeling legs. Then out of the blue appeared a ray of light followed by bubbling in the cool water. Caught in my reflection was a tail, with golden, velvet scales glimmering in the shining, summertime sunbeams. Overwhelmed by the pure thought, I gazed at my new aqua creation; my tail. Was I dreaming? No. I was a mythical creature. A mermaid!

Shauna Murney (8)
St Anselm's Catholic Primary School, Wandsworth

Dinky's Wormhole

There once was an alien on Pluto, the coldest planet, called Dinky. He was yellow and blobby and moved on wheels instead of legs. One day, he fell down a wormhole, was transported to Mercury, the hottest planet. While he sat there getting used to the heat, Winky, another alien, appeared. They plated in the sand dunes. Suddenly, a gang of aliens called The Biters began to shoot lasers. Dinky knew this was a dangerous place and felt scared for his friend. He grabbed Winky's hand and pulled him to the wormhole, back to safe Pluto. They were transported!

Elizabeth Margaret Patricia Armitage (9)
St Anselm's Catholic Primary School, Wandsworth

The Land Of Fuzzy Creatures

Once there was a monster who woke up in a new land. The land was called 'The Land of Fuzzy Creatures'. It was amazing! So the monster, named Miss Fuzzy Lady, went outside to discover it. She saw trees hanging down as if they were ready to grab her; she saw lots and lots of other creatures around. Those creatures were nice. But suddenly, their enemies came and invaded them. Eventually, their soldiers defeated them. It was a victory for the good creatures. By the end, Miss Fuzzy Lady lived happily in this extraordinary land.

Chloé Sachet-Dufraisse (8)

St Anselm's Catholic Primary School, Wandsworth

Robot Attack

Trudging along the hot beach, Hither-Gen mourned his lost son. He turned to see a research tower, not knowing they were tracking him. Just then, he heard a rustle behind a tree, and the clanking of metal. Rushing towards him was a robot with guns. This robot was more terrifying than the ones on his home planet, Mars. Suddenly, it started shooting! He tried to tame it at first, but it didn't work, so he shape-shifted into a bug. The robot shot a net towards him and Hither-Gen quickly changed into a parrot and escaped over the tropical trees.

Cormac Haspel (8)
St Anselm's Catholic Primary School, Wandsworth

Plod And The Mighty Handcuff Dropper

Plod, from Venus, trudged along the rocky, stony path while he whistled, making him in a good mood. He saw a dragon on the floor, crying out for help. Plod felt sorry for the dragon, so he went to heal him. He noticed a red-hot, circular trap, clamping his legs together. It was almost like he was handcuffed. Suddenly, Plod noticed a massive handcuff coming to hit him! He ran away from the handcuff but the handcuff was going at an amazing speed. Suddenly, millions of handcuffs fell out of the sky, trying to hit him. 'Oops!' he shouted.

Johnny Gardner (9)
St Anselm's Catholic Primary School, Wandsworth

Snot Eyes And The Robot

There was a superhero who was as fierce as an angry bull. His name was Snot Eyes! He was in a battle against the Robot Federation, who were trying to destroy the planet Zog. He fought gallantly by firing snot out of his glaring eyes and blinding them. For three days he battled the robots until there was no snot left. He had demolished an army which would have filled ten football pitches. There was one droid left. Instead of killing it, he made it his servant, who gave him tea and cake every day while he saved the world.

Thomas Hulett (8)
St Anselm's Catholic Primary School, Wandsworth

Touch The Sun

Sprang pushed the door open, and jumped onto the sofa, which was yellow just like him. He was just about to fall asleep, when something caught his eye. He had noticed a white patch in the sofa. Sprang stood up to fix it, but it disappeared! The very confused alien was about to cover his mouth with his hand when, what a surprise, Sprang observed that it was white! He bounced straight out of the house, out of the front garden and onto the street. All his friends were there! Sprang jumped up, touched the sun and regained his colour!

Blanche Symington (8)

St Anselm's Catholic Primary School, Wandsworth

Plurina Gets Captured!

Once upon a time there lived a young mermaid called Plurina. She was only five when she got captured by her auntie. Her auntie was called Melissa. Melissa was evil, she captured young Plurina and didn't feed her for five days at all, until Plurina escaped. She hid in a cave for one week until she was strong again, strong enough to get back to her home. She was a princess after all, so her father sent the guards to find her auntie. It only took one day to find her so they threw her in their large kingdom's prison.

Raphaelle Olivia Treneman (8)

St Anselm's Catholic Primary School, Wandsworth

I'm Not Perfect

I'm green like a courgette but my legs are tiny like a duck. Call me Zooking Ducking Smuke as my smile will make you happy. I have a captivating smile, that's why people want me to be their pet. Although, I'm afraid that some people may not like me because I'm not perfect. Believe it or not, I hate this feeling, I need to accept that I'm one of the unique creatures that God created. Be brave and have the courage to say *I love myself* and in turn people will care, comfort and love me too!

Marianne Amate (9)
St Anselm's Catholic Primary School, Wandsworth

The Genius Monster Kid

There was once a boy called Jakle. Jakle was a genius when he was two years old. He went to Minosaur Primary School and while he was walking to school, he saw his evil enemy, Buck, but his nickname is Blood Red. Buck punched Jakle in his tummy and vomited. When Jakle went home, his nose was bleeding because he pushed Buck out of the way. So the next day, he built a robot and the robot made Buck cry, and that was Jakle's bodyguard forever. Buck never bullied Jakle ever again. Jakle lived a good life again!

Ava Boaten (9)
St Anselm's Catholic Primary School, Wandsworth

Half Of The Enemy!

Once upon a time, in a galaxy called Quidlop, on a small planet called Gilfplood, there lived a big alien called Klodpork. Klodpork lived a happy life until his arch-enemy, Doolpflig, attacked his home. Klodpork knew what to do. There was a thunder-crashing landing from the sky. Suddenly, with quick reflexes, Klodpork shape-shifted into a flamethrower and set Doolpflig on fire. But then, what seemed impossible, Doolpflig emerged from the flames and shot Klodpork! There lying on the floor was a dead, lifeless Klodpork.

Finn Mulcahy (9)

St Anselm's Catholic Primary School, Wandsworth

Lord Problem

Once upon a time there lived a monster called Gobblelord. He lived in a gloomy, dark cave near a castle on Lord Land. Seeing as he was in Lord Land, he ate lords for lunch and supper. Luckily for Gobblelord, he was a shape-shifter so he could collect the lords. One day, there were no more lords left and Gobblelord was starving. A few days later, a ripped scroll appeared at the front door. Standing beside the scroll was a little boy. Gobblelord was about to laser the boy but the boy took him to a new land with lords.

Isabel Stahel (9)
St Anselm's Catholic Primary School, Wandsworth

Jags' Adventure

Excited, elated, scared, Jags woke up. Today was his favourite day as he could disguise himself as a teacher and go into a school. Today was Mufti Day. He started by painting his big, thick body peach. After that, he managed to fit a short, stubby tie around his neck. He covered his short, little wings on his head with a hat. The hardest things to disguise were his legs as they were dark blue tentacles. He squashed them into some trousers that he had stolen. He smiled, today was the day he got to feast on tasty children.

Thomas Pike (8)
St Anselm's Catholic Primary School, Wandsworth

Flanko's Game

Flanko was a quick and observant creature, always ready for anything. He was playing Quick Ball, a game where you grabbed the ball with your feet and ran really fast to the pit, while other opponents tried to hit the ball off you. With two heads, Flanko could see both in front and behind, making him a really good player. Flanko was losing. As a player tried to hit the ball, he hit Flanko and he went flying into an iron box. He was trapped! Flanko had to work out how to escape if he wanted to win the game!

Alfie Henry Pennington (9)
St Anselm's Catholic Primary School, Wandsworth

Enemies

When Stripezesher was on his journey home from an everlasting hunt, he caught sight of the familiar bodies. He wasn't especially sure who the people in his sight were. As he started to walk over to the bodies, while gazing at them, he noticed them running towards him! Suddenly, he recognised them! They were his darkest enemies, Menoture and Sian! He ran away from them knowing he could not win two on one, but both of them could fly, meaning he was caught easily! Before he knew it, he was on the floor, dead.

Charles Wilson (9)

St Anselm's Catholic Primary School, Wandsworth

Igneel And The Village

Igneel wandered past the joyful mountains with his four horse-like hooves and hawk-like talons, roasting his pig.

'This is strange, I haven't seen a bustling doll village in Zentopai! Have I?'

Thump, thump! he heard.

'That means...Thruple with his giant ear wings.'

But Thruple was far; he had about twenty-three minutes. He found his favourite creature, the strongest, a kid Niusa, who had fire powers.

'Leave, all of you!'

Thump, thump!

He flew away, it was his enemy, the... Monkey! He transformed into a cloud and shot fire at the monkey. Niusa helped Ignell. The monkey came. They fought fiercely.

Kolade Alli (10)
St Helen's RC Primary School, Brixton

Dark Jelaten

Dark Jelaten was cheerfully walking around the forest feeling very hot. As he was walking through, he heard a loud, crazy sound. It was two troublesome teenagers skateboarding with fire boards. Dark Jelaten used his vomiting powers to slime them away, and as he took care of the mess he made, nine more teenagers suddenly appeared, throwing swords and knives. Dark Jelaten didn't like this and was really angry, and used his mega vomiting powers and blew all of the awkward teenagers away. Dark Jelaten thought long and hard, he decided to give up on sliming teenagers and go home.

Samuel O Ajayi (9)
St Helen's RC Primary School, Brixton

Heartoress And The Troublemaking Trolls

Heartoress trotted around the bustling village on her four pig's legs, looking for troublemaking trolls. All of a sudden, her hair sensed a problem and stuck up like a lightning bolt! That meant one thing, trouble! Heartoress heated up her left eye ready to zap. A few seconds later, Heartoress found a person that was in trouble. She was with the troublemaking trolls; Heartoress' worst enemies. She quickly zapped them! Helpful Heartoress told the young lady to never listen to the ugly trolls. It was a fun day zapping trolls. Heartoress prayed for another day like it.

Lillyrose Tuswa (9)
St Helen's RC Primary School, Brixton

Luther And The Dazzling Demon

His face was as red as blood; he buckled along in loneliness. He mysteriously started to sweat. His large black wings started to drop. Luther's dotted eyes began to close gently in the dark. He passed out like a baby, and woke up on his four rectangular legs. Without delay, his long, lion-like tail started shaking in fear. A fly gazed on top of him. Luther ran as if he'd had a nightmare. Screaming in fear, he buckled and tripped.
'Leave me alone, you small killer!'
With his four legs, he transformed into a horse, running with dark fear.

Jaden Frempong (10)
St Helen's RC Primary School, Brixton

Triceptor The Great!

Triceptor trod through the Tritartic with his giraffe-like feet. He then looked around with all his twenty eyes. He was eating animals that came to the Tritartic so no one could destroy his beloved land. Then he saw humans! Triceptor got furious. He used his laser eyes, but they dodged it. He had a back-up power. Mind control power! He controlled their minds and sent them away. It was then, when reinforcements came marching over the headland, Triceptor realised they hadn't brought any defences, so he used his dangerous laser eyes. He destroyed all of them.

Henok Ghebrihiwot Tecle (10)
St Helen's RC Primary School, Brixton

TripledEyed

TripledEyed roamed around. TripledEyed realised that this was not his home. TripledEyed thought so hard he actually forgot what he was thinking about. He heard a bird cry, so he used his gogo boots to see what it was.

'Oh no, it's my enemy, Eagle.'

TripledEyed camouflaged in the bushes. He didn't know what to do next. He thought so deeply.

'Yes, I can use my Minotaur horns to destroy Eagle! What a great plan.'

TripledEyed took a shot and hit Eagle. TripledEyed was proud, but still didn't know the way back home.

Olubisi Olubode (10)

St Helen's RC Primary School, Brixton

Unidragon's Dream

Unidragon woke up with a shiver down her spine. She realised she was in the middle of nowhere. Suddenly, her magical horn started flashing red. That meant the devil-eyed dolphins were coming. As quick as a flash, Unidragon ran to them and eventually turned them into stone. After that, more dangerous dolphins came and Unidragon ran away. She sprinted as quick as a leopard in a race. It was getting dark. Unidragon was trying to find a place she could take a nap. Unidragon dreamed about evil dolphins. Suddenly, Unidragon woke up. Her horn flashed dark red. Danger!

Asia Mieszczakowska (10)
St Helen's RC Primary School, Brixton

Electra And The Adventure

Electra walked with her two small feet and saw that she was in the wrong place. Suddenly, the sun came out and she couldn't happily electrocute people. She went to the deep end of the cave and found some people to electrocute in darkness. She couldn't electric shock people outside because the sun was in the way. But then the sun went away and she was pretty happy that the sun went away. She said, 'I have to electric shock people because the sun will come out again and I can't electrocute them.' So they turned and she electrocuted them.

Blanca Santeugini (10)
St Helen's RC Primary School, Brixton

The Ping Forest

Allys were walking in a strange place. They didn't know where they were going. They were so scared that they began to scream. So they used their map, which was on the back of their heads. The only reason was if Sally and Ally didn't know the postcode. After that, they were trying really hard until they saw an animal. Sally and Ally were trying to communicate with the animal. Then the animal made a noise and they didn't know what to do next. Then the animal's mum called him so the animal went. Just from that moment, they're happy.

Mya Pontes (10)
St Helen's RC Primary School, Brixton

Lanky And The Creepy Aliens

Lanky wandered around the middle of nowhere. He had no idea where he was. He had nothing to do! Lanky used his super hearing to sense if there was any danger about. He heard voices in the far distance. What could it be? Could it be people? No! It was aliens! They came closer, and closer to Lanky. He ran as fast as a cheetah because he was so scared! Then, he stopped running and remembered he had superpowers. So he used his lasers to blast the creepy aliens. The aliens stood up and pushed Lanky... Who would win?

Justin Dafê (10)

St Helen's RC Primary School, Brixton

Joker Fetty Vs Rolsefúongon

I realised I was walking in my enemy's park. I panicked! My heart was pounding like a bongo drum. I started warming up the lasers at the back of my blue eyeballs. As I came running down the path like a cheetah, I turned and saw my enemy, Rolsefúongon. He sprayed out toothpaste and it went all around me. I burnt him, but he shot out more toothpaste! Then I controlled his brain and then we both teleported to a big, gushing waterfall. I fainted like a baby. Would this be the end for me?

Jean Yves Dorgeles Zehia (10)
St Helen's RC Primary School, Brixton

Joker Fetty

I entered a weird place and saw a statue of my crazy enemy, Joker Fetty. I drank some of my magical toothpaste to protect myself from danger. Joker Fetty randomly popped around the corner. He shot lasers, but I ducked. I shot toothpaste and captured him. I ran home but my door was locked, I probably lost my key. I stretched my neck and saw a bunch of bees. They looked at me fiercely. They started chasing me, I ran as fast as I could like a strong lion. How crazy am I? I literally have no strong smart brains!

Sean Diego Encalada Obaco (10)
St Helen's RC Primary School, Brixton

Brock And The Pigs

Brock Lesnar was calmly walking through the tiny Jonclog forest when he saw a family of fat pigs. His small tail wiggled, they broke into his house. He hid behind a tree - very scared. Brock was in the dark shadow of the tree. He then panicked and shot lasers out from his big eyes. They noticed! He recovered by aiming at the pigs and killed them all. He was happy because he got cooked pork. He walked down to the small village and a pig was behind him. He shot the pig, who dropped sadly to the green grass.

Luis Coelho (10)
St Helen's RC Primary School, Brixton

Dr Furball And The Injection Of Horror

Dr Furball was on another adventure. Dr Furball had flown into the forest. There were many creatures like the Bearded-Butchers, the Too-Toos and, deadliest of them all and also Dr Furball's enemy, Sharktooth. Dr Furball found a cave to take shelter. Suddenly, he saw a big shadow. It's Sharktooth! Dr Furball ran at Sharktooth and Sharktooth knocked him out. When Dr Furball woke up, he was in a laboratory. Sharktooth was getting an injection ready. Dr Furball pretended to be asleep. Sharktooth came to put the injection in. Dr Furball sucked his blood and killed him. Hooray for Dr Furball!

Bill McCarthy (8)
St Mary Magdalen's Catholic Primary School, London

Tlingbot And Ellie

Tlingbot was walking around his new house on Pluto when he spotted Ellie the eagle, his arch-enemy. Tlingbot walked backwards, but accidentally fell over and made a loud *bang!*
Oh no, he thought. Ellie swooped down to catch him, but missed. Tlingbot kept running as fast as his little legs could carry him.
There's a corner coming up soon, I'll turn there, he thought. When the corner came up, he turned the corner and hid behind a tree. Ellie did not see the corner and flew straight past it.
'Phew, I am safe,' said Tlingbot.
Tlingbot's safe, for now...

Lavinia Cora Fia Hopkins (9)
St Mary Magdalen's Catholic Primary School, London

Thimble And The Not-So-Lost Garden

Where am I? pondered Thimble glumly. The last thing she remembered was casually walking on the desk and then she stepped out the window and everything went dark. She opened her eyes and wished she hadn't. Huge orange eyes stared around her. Then she remembered she was invisible. She looked around and then realised she wasn't invisible. She looked around and then realised she wasn't invisible! She let her wings fly and swooped over the fence. The creature was a cat! The cat pounced beside her and she glided back down to the window, sluggishly crawled inside and fainted.

Lukas Glasheen (9)
St Mary Magdalen's Catholic Primary School, London

The Vegetarian Raptor

The Raptor sped along through the black sand desert on his two mechanical feet, the red sun beating down hard on his metallic back. He was going to his friend's house for lunch and he was late! Suddenly, he was ambushed by laser beans that jumped out of a nearby plutonium cactus. They fired blinding rainbow-coloured lasers. With all his might, the Raptor jumped thirty feet high and pointed his mini flamethrower arm at the laser beans. Then he cooked them to death and said, 'That'll be today's lunch!'

Then, with great agility, he ran to his friend's house.

Edward Jones (9)
St Mary Magdalen's Catholic Primary School, London

The Lost Dugbog

It was midnight. Angle the dugbog was scared. She had lost her family. Her tiny paws trudged along the dusty desert, through the jungle, but Angle still couldn't find home.

'I miss home,' she moaned.

Suddenly, there was a big thud. How that thud made her jump! She stepped closer and closer until she found a tiny circular gemstone.

'What is this?' she asked herself curiously.

It suddenly lit up. In front of her was the home she had lost. She was so happy. She looked around for her parents. They were all there waiting for her to return.

Brisa Willoughby (9)

St Mary Magdalen's Catholic Primary School, London

The Collapsed Bridge

Once, there was a mysterious creature who was born in Canada. She lived in a village with her family. Her name was Miana. When she was ten, the village bridge collapsed. Without the bridge, the villagers couldn't cross the river to harvest the crops. Miana and her sister, Niana, built a new bridge. They cut down some trees and collected a lot of vines and built the bridge.

'Hip, hip, hooray!'

All the villagers were happy now they could cross the bridge and harvest the crops for food.

They rewarded the sisters by making them the captains of the village!

Maaira Hussain (9)

St Mary Magdalen's Catholic Primary School, London

Mr Spot And The Magic Bracelet

Mr Spot left his house.

'I can't miss this!' he said to himself, 'Not with my magic bracelet.'

Mr Spot threw the house keys down the well.

'I won't be needing those when I go to live in the haunted hotel!'

He looked down at his arm.

'Now,' he said, 'I will just press the button on my magic bracelet to teleport me to the haunted hotel and... what? It's gone! The bracelet is gone! I can't believe it! I must have left it at home! Plus, the key is thrown down the deep well! Oh, how silly of me.'

Saoirse Chandler (8)
St Mary Magdalen's Catholic Primary School, London

The Story of Jeddy and Jubby's Friendship

Jubby is an alien from Pweni in Pluto. One day, he met another alien called Jeddy. Jeddy and Jubby went to buy some jelly. Jeddy offered to carry Jubby's jelly, so he did, but instead of carrying the jelly, he threw it in Jubby's face! That's when Jubby knew Jeddy was a bully and he ran home to his mum. Jeddy kept bullying Jubby for years and he ran to his mum every time. Until one time when Jeddy crashed his spaceship into Jubby's on purpose. Then he realised what he did was wrong and he said, 'Sorry, BFFs forever?'

Sadhbh Fahy (8)
St Mary Magdalen's Catholic Primary School, London

The Day Of Doom

With a thud, Babeeeee landed in the middle of Antarctica. For a few minutes, he lay there not knowing what to do. When finally getting up, he realised that he was surrounded by the Plutonians who were his enemies. Babeeeee felt a shiver down his spine. He did not know what to do so he stood there, knowing that the Plutonians would attack. After four minutes of dreaded silence, some Plutonians charged at him and started tugging him along. Next, Babeeeee found himself under a cliff, trying to get out but failing until he found a way out.

David William Derfinak (9)

St Mary Magdalen's Catholic Primary School, London

Battle Of Survival

One tragic day, a guy called Paul lost a battle against Sideboard and he got sucked into a blackhole, and when he was an inch away he threw Slugbat in a jar to safety, so he didn't get sucked into the blackhole. Then Slugbat hopped away to Paul's son, Eli, and told him about his father and Eli got really mad and he got an army of Slugbats and trained them to defeat Sideboard, and his army they met. Then Eli said, 'Attack!' and Sideboard said, 'Attack!' and they had a big war. Eli won his father's freedom.

Elliot Laurence Kinsella (8)
St Mary Magdalen's Catholic Primary School, London

Bob Gets A Suit

Bob slid along the boiling-hot desert in Jedha. His slimy feet weren't a good match for the hot deserts of Jedha. Bob wished he could get back to his home in Leides, that's where the perfect match for his feet were. Suddenly, he stumbled across a very mysterious suit. It looked like it could fly. He remembered where he crashed into the desert. So he tried the high-tech suit on. It was the perfect fit for him. He saw some buttons and they weren't complex like all buttons. There was backwards, forwards and fly. So he flew home.

Shane Kenny (8)
St Mary Magdalen's Catholic Primary School, London

Gorg

Gorg is an alien from a land unknown. When he was born his parents threw him away because he was too weak. But one day, he discovered Earth. To everyone it was a mystery, what this thing was. One day, he interrupted an interview with the Queen so he could let everybody know who he was. The trouble was, he spoke in Shnoz. When he finished, someone translated it because they knew Shnoz. After the interview, everyone was friends with him. After that, he quickly went back to Shnozville, told everyone about Earth and they invaded!

TJ Maciejewski (9)
St Mary Magdalen's Catholic Primary School, London

Minop's Visit To Earth

Minop was just launched by a rocket to Earth. Minop found himself being pushed out of the rocket.He did not know whether to run back to the rocket or to run somewhere on Earth. He decided to run back to the rocket but it was too late! A human had already seen him. Minop started running but he ran straight into a human! The humans shouted, 'Let's have a battle with this alien monster!'

His friends came and Minop called his friends too. They had a long, long battle and at last, the Venus monsters had won!

Maja Paliga (9)

St Mary Magdalen's Catholic Primary School, London

Untitled

There once was a man called John who went into space. One day, a big space storm arose from where nobody knows and hit the space shuttle. It was a disaster. They crash-landed on Mars, but there was something even worse than that! John looked at his used-to-be human body, but now it was a combination of a vampire with electrons! In his mind, he was thinking, *What should I do?* He thought day and night until he had an idea; since he was also made of electrons, he could power up his space shuttle. He was home.

Tonatiuh Fiorini (9)
St Mary Magdalen's Catholic Primary School, London

Max The Dead Devil

On a faraway planet called Pluto lived a dragon called Oliv. She was kind and not like the other dragons she lived with. One day, when she was going to get some food, she saw a dragon she hadn't seen before. Its name was Max and he was evil. Since Oliv saw Max, she was trying to kill him, but it never worked. At last, she thought she should set a trap in front of Max's creepy den. When Max was coming out of his den to destroy Oliv and other people, he fell into the trap and died.

Samiha Sohail (8)

St Mary Magdalen's Catholic Primary School, London

Tim

My creature is called Tim. He is ten years old, he is small but he is also vicious. Unfortunately, he doesn't have a big tail so this makes him very naughty. He decided he didn't want to be angry. He went online and looked for a tail enlarger. He waited for the postman to bring it. when it arrived, he pit it around his tail and pumped and pulled. His tail was now longer, he was the happiest creature! He showed his long tail to everyone and was not vicious or angry any more.

Tyler Davidson Wanjiru (9)
St Mary Magdalen's Catholic Primary School, London

The Bullies

Snuffles sniffed. He could sense the smell of Arobitey but he couldn't work out where it was coming from.

'Ah, I wonder where he is!'

Meanwhile, hiding behind the wall was Arobitey and his gang.

'Stop there mister,' barked Arobitey to Snuffles.

'Right, just remember, you tell no one about this, otherwise you're in big trouble!' remarked one of Arobitey's gang.

'Hey! I was supposed to say that,' whispered Arobitey.

'No, when we planned this, you said-'

'What you gonna do?' begged Snuffles.

'We're gonna chuck you in the dustbin and- '

'Sssh, don't tell him.'

'Mum! Help!' screamed Snuffles.

Emily Sophia Lysons (10)
St Olave's Preparatory School, New Eltham

Neptune Is My Home

'Help me,' cried Nepolian, 'Neptune is my home.'
No one answered, he was on Jupiter because he
got blown off Neptune by one of its strong winds.
Now he was battling to get through the storm.
Suddenly, he got blown right off Jupiter.
'Arghhhh!' Nepolian cried.
A few hours later, Nepolian landed on a rather
hard object.
'Ouch,' he said when he landed.
'Hello,' said a strange bug, 'welcome to the moon.'
'I need help,' said Nepolian.
'OK,' said the moon bug.
So they made a rocket and blasted Nepolian into
space. He landed safely on Neptune and was
happy.

Emilia Grace Morgan (10)
St Olave's Preparatory School, New Eltham

Dino-Terror!

Speed zoomed out of his bed. How could he forget Papa's birthday? Mama, Speed and Zoom sung 'Happy Birthday' to Papa. *Stomp! Stamp!* 'What was that?' asked Zoom.

It was T-Rex who was always terrorising Dino planet. Speed would not let his ruin Papa's birthday so they all leapt up to save the day! They ran 60mph. Then leapt on T-Rex. Zoom, Mama and Papa held T-Rex still then Speed ran around T-Rex's legs, then *kaboom!* T-Rex fell to the ground. Later, the dino police came and congratulated them. Papa said humbly, 'That was the best birthday.'

Adam Barbe (9)
St Olave's Preparatory School, New Eltham

Naughty Devil Bat!

There lived a monster called Devil Bat. He could be invisible and change into something or someone; a shape-shifter.

Every Halloween he changed into the scariest monster and frightened lots of children until they cried.

The children of Devil Town decided to teach Devil Bat a lesson. There was something that Devil Bat hated, and that was clowns!

They waited quietly and as Devil Bat approached the town, all the children dressed as clowns and leapt out of the trees.

Devil Bat was extremely scared! Next Halloween, Devil Bat shape-shifted into a flower which was beautiful - everyone loved him.

Mia Alexandra Wilks (8)

St Olave's Preparatory School, New Eltham

Mars

The rocket crashed onto Mars rapidly. Tim and Bob were going to be the first people to walk on the rocky red planet. Just then, Bob saw a ten-eyed, towering, hairy, big-mouthed, scary monster.

'There's a Martian!' shouted Bob, as Tim turned around.

The gigantic monster opened its eyes and stood there looking weirdly at them. Then more of them appeared on the dark, misty planet. Soon, hundreds of monsters were surrounding them.

'I think they want our food,' said Tim, worried.

'I think we should go into our secure rocket where it is safe,' said Bob, terrified.

Ajmal Malique (9)
St Olave's Preparatory School, New Eltham

Super Slik Destroys Evil Doctor Smith

Slik Strong is from planet Oriel where men are strong with X-ray eyes and travel in supersonic automobile spaceships. One day, Slik received an urgent letter from Tom who lived on Planet Earth. Slik swiftly jumped into his automobile and zoomed across the galaxy and landed at Tom's home. Tom was very grateful and excited to see his hero, Slik. Tom said, 'Doctor Smith has stolen from us and is in the pub.'
Slik got to the pub and used his X-ray eyes to locate Doctor Smith, and with his strength he returned the stolen goods to a grateful Tom.

Zuriel Elueme (9)

St Olave's Preparatory School, New Eltham

It Fell On Mars!

Plankton and Uranus had decided that they should busy themselves doing something, so they decided they should make an invention. Plankton and Uranus gathered some pieces and started making. Suddenly, there was a big, fat crash! It had landed right behind Uranus. First, they both ignored it, but then they thought they could put it in their invention. They went over to it and then thought it was too big, but they did not know what it was. They lifted it up and took it over to their invention. 'What has landed on my only planet?'
'It is Mars!'

Darcey Baxter (9)
St Olave's Preparatory School, New Eltham

Girl Power

One day, Cutaso was combing her luscious hair when suddenly, in the mirror, she saw a peculiar face with a mask on. She knew at once who it was. It was Snortlops! Cutaso hated Snortlops. He came over and said, 'Oi, get out of my way!'
Cutaso didn't like him bossing creatures around. She decided she would teach him a lesson by gathering all of the other creatures and telling them to attack the evil Snortlops. They all charged at him. Snortlops was so scared that he actually ran away! Cutaso became everyone's favourite hero! Snortlops was never seen again!

Rania Kochhar (10)
St Olave's Preparatory School, New Eltham

Trying To Get Out!

As Fuzzy was trudging along, he had an idea. He was going to go and see his friends in the Land of Roses, where flowers grew even in the winter and where rivers glistened like the evening sunset! The next day, at the crack of dawn, Fuzzy was off. Walking over hills of sand and mountains of grass until he got to a huge sign saying: *Gates To Skillful Senses Land*, where Fuzzy lived. There were two big, tough guards standing there.

One said, 'You can't get out.'

Fuzzy dived forward and reached for a pole which came down. *Bang!*

Mia Griffiths (10)
St Olave's Preparatory School, New Eltham

It's Just A Dream

Strawberry Slug was just strolling along until he realised he was dreaming! He tried hard to wake himself up but it was no use!

So he thought, *I can do whatever I want because I'm in a dream.*

First he travelled to a planet called Earth and spoke to the humans, then he flew as high as the mutant bird. Later on he realised he'd never get to see his family again because he's stuck in this dream.

So he thought, *I'll make a portal to get myself out of here.*

The portal was done just in time for breakfast.

Qasim Ahmed (9)
St Olave's Preparatory School, New Eltham

Skiddy Vs Slidey

There once lived a monster; his name was Skiddy.
All he loved to do was play football. He played for
his local football team. He was the best on the
team. Then a new monster came onto the team.
His name was Slidey. Every game, Skiddy was a
substitute. One day, Skiddy had enough and said
to his coach, 'If I don't start in the next game - I will
quit!'
The next game, Skiddy started the match instead
of Slidey. Slidey became cross. However, Skiddy
scored the winning goal, Slidey decided it's best to
be friends rather than enemies.

Ethan Daley (10)

St Olave's Preparatory School, New Eltham

The Red Monster

Fiftoe searched for the Red Monster and found a track. Miraculously, it led to the monster. Fiftoe was ready to destroy him. He concluded he needed Alli to help him. so on his radio he contacted Alli by Fizzflop air. They tried to destroy him but it didn't work. Alli decided to walk backwards around planet Fizzflop; trailing behind was the monster Fiftoe, and Alli hid behind a rock. He walked on. Alli walked into his house and found a catapult! Alli tumbled into the sky and he blinded the monster. The Red Monster walked into a rock and crashed!

Sophia Zoryana Smith (10)
St Olave's Preparatory School, New Eltham

The Penguin Show

No one knows where Ting came from, because he was invisible to humans. It was only animals that could see him. So Ting hung out at the zoo. He was orange with pink spots so totally different from the other animals. Ting's favourite animals were the penguins. How he wished he could swim. So his best friend, Pepper the penguin, taught him. Soon he was an expert so he could do the shows with them. He glided, twisting and turning in the pool. When the crowd cheered, Ting jumped with glee. Together, Ting and Pepper, were a team in celebration.

Sofia Chhatlani (9)
St Olave's Preparatory School, New Eltham

The Bubble Beast!

The Bubble Beast was made by a crazy professor. The Bubble Beast, BB for short, had fifty small bubbles for arms and a hundred small bubbles for feet, and a gigantic bubble for his body. One day, the crazy professor opened the window, oh no! Suddenly, BB blew far, far away. BB went so high that he went through the clouds; the candyfloss clouds gave him a beard! Uh-oh! Then came the birds with their sharp beaks! *Peck, peck, pop, pop!* BB fell down, down, down. As quick as a flash, BB fell into a rose garden. Bye BB.

Mia-Rainbow O'Regan (9)
St Olave's Preparatory School, New Eltham

Monster Mystery

A monster was spotted in London. This put the public in a state of panic. The monster was green, the size of a car and reeked. It was an urgent matter which needs to be sorted out. The army had been mobilised. There were tanks and machine guns at the police's command. The monster was easily the ugliest thing we had ever seen. The army lined up in front of the monster. It slowly lumbered away from us, bullets bouncing off. It took an hour before we penetrated its skin and finally killed it by a missile through the eye.

Henry Wygas (10)
St Olave's Preparatory School, New Eltham

Soggy Saves The Day

Soggy was a blue monster who could make water appear from nowhere. He lived in the Sahara Desert. Salty the camel was mean and took all the water. One day, Salty drank all the water at the oasis. A very thirsty explorer arrived, needing water, but there was none. The explorer was scared he would die without any water. Luckily, Soggy saw what Salty had done. He came over to the explorer and made water to save the man's life. The man was a prince and made Soggy into a knight called Sir Soggy the Wet, to say thank you.

Matthew Pownall (9)

St Olave's Preparatory School, New Eltham

The Mission

Derrick was a normal robot on his home planet, Scalion. Today, it was going to be a hard day. Derrick overheard two other robots saying that the Polaroid had a new glitch that was being unleashed against Scalion. Derrick was a mechanic so he built a pod which was going to catapult into their airship. So he set up the catapult and in five seconds he was in the airship! He was as quiet as a mouse. He destroyed the glitch and he returned to his planet. He was a hero! Then he returned to his mechanic shop.

Harry James Green (10)
St Olave's Preparatory School, New Eltham

160

Jump Of Life

There once lived a shape-shifter. He loved jumping, so he started to practice. Soon he was picked to have a jump-off with his nemesis, Sticky Tongue John. They used to be friends but then they had an argument and they never saw each other until that day. It was off, the final battle. It was who could get the highest in a hundred bounces. Sticky Tongue John started bravely, he felt proud of himself as he walked up. It was over like that. It was Simon next, somehow he did not want to go, but he did...

Christopher Thomas (10)
St Olave's Preparatory School, New Eltham

Snif's Adventure

Snif is about to leave his home, Mars, to travel to Gon, but he saw two strange creatures outside his house. He looked at his watch and he was late for his ship to Gon. Snif now, as you guess, was running so fast he could hear his heart beating as he made his way to the ship in time before the ship took off. But the two strange creatures from earlier, Sape and Nape, followed Snif on the ship to Gon to get their revenge on Snif for getting them in jail. Hopefully Snif will make it alive!

Ben Fowler (10)
St Olave's Preparatory School, New Eltham

The Final Battle

Fuzzy Bee woke up hearing about Lava Bee wanting to attack him. He had been planning it so he took over the sea and turned it into lava. Fuzzy Bee had a plan. His plan was to kill him with his weakness, water! So that is what he did. Lava Bee started, when they settled the fight by attacking straight. Fuzzy Bee went to plan. He got as much water as possible and told everyone to hold one bucket each and then throw it at the enemies. Fuzzy Bee threw the bucket of water on Lava Bee and finally won!

Dhillon Blaggan (10)
St Olave's Preparatory School, New Eltham

YoungWriters
Est.1991

YOUNG WRITERS
INFORMATION

We hope you have enjoyed reading this book – and
that you will continue to in the coming years.

If you're a young writer who enjoys reading and creative
writing, or the parent of an enthusiastic poet or story writer,
do visit our website **www.youngwriters.co.uk**. Here you will
find free competitions, workshops and games, as well as
recommended reads, a poetry glossary and our blog.

If you would like to order further copies of this book,
or any of our other titles, then please give us
a call or visit **www.youngwriters.co.uk**.

Young Writers
Remus House
Coltsfoot Drive
Peterborough
PE2 9BF
(01733) 890066
info@youngwriters.co.uk